MATHNET™ CASEBOOK

#3 *The Case of the Willing Parrot*

By David D. Connell and Jim Thurman

Illustrated by Danny O'Leary

Scientific
BOOKS FOR YOUNG READERS
American

Children's Television Workshop

W. H. Freeman/New York

Scientific American Books for Young Readers
is an imprint of W.H. Freeman and Company,
41 Madison Avenue, New York, New York 10010

On **MATHNET**, the role of George Frankly is played
by Joe Howard; the role of Kate Monday
is played by Beverly Leech.

Cover photo of Joe Howard © CTW/Richard Termine

Illustrated by Danny O'Leary

Activities by Richard Chevat

Activity illustrations by Lynn Brunelle

Library of Congress Cataloging-in-Publication Data

Connell, David D.

The Case of the Willing Parrot: Mathnet, Casebook/by David D. Connell and Jim Thurman.

p. cm.

Summary: Mathnet detectives Kate Monday and George Frankly use math skills to solve the mystery of where deceased comic Fatty Tissue hid his fortune.

ISBN 0-7167-6528-4 (hard).—ISBN 0-7167-6522-5 (soft)

[1. Parrot—Fiction. 2. Mathematics—Fiction. 3. Mystery and detective stories.] I. Thurman, Jim, ill. II. Title.

PZ7.C761853Cas 1994

[Fic]—dc20   93-29321

                                                    CIP

                                                    AC

Printed in the United States of America
10 9 8 7 6 5 4 3 2 1

CHAPTER

1

It was 9:43 A.M. when Kate Monday walked out of the spring sunshine into Mathnet HQ. As she opened the door to her office, she saw George Frankly, her partner, already hard at work. Then Kate looked closer. She saw that George wasn't working on a case. He was playing with a model train.

"Wooo-wooooo," Kate said, imitating a train whistle. "Good morning, Casey Jones."

"Oh, it's you, Kate," George said, smiling distractedly.

"George, why are you doing whatever it is you're doing?"

"I'm building an H.O. gauge model train, Kate," George said. "It's for my brother's little boy."

"Your nephew?" Kate asked.

George thought a moment. "Yeah, I guess that *would* make him my nephew." He picked up the caboose and displayed it proudly. "It's a beauty, isn't it, Kate?"

"A beauty, all right," Kate agreed.

"Of course, you probably wouldn't appreciate it because you were never a little boy," George made the mistake of adding.

Kate stared at her partner in disbelief.

George tried again. "I mean, you were probably a little girl. Little girls don't play with trains. They play with, you know, dolls."

Kate rolled her eyes. "George, I *had* an electric train when I was a kid," she said. "I also had a baseball glove and a hockey stick!"

"Boy, I wish I'd lived next door to you," George said wistfully. "We could have played together."

Kate shook her head and looked back at the train set-up. "My train wasn't an H.O., though. What does H.O. mean, anyway?"

George held up the caboose. "H.O. *gauge*, Kate. It's a scale used to make model trains. It means that this caboose is one eighty-seventh the size of a real one. Model trains come in all different sizes, so they're labeled by the gauge. That way you know which ones will fit your set."

Kate smiled. "Can't get away from mathematics even when you're relaxing, can you, George?" she teased.

"Guess not," George replied. A moment later he was bent over the train set again, fitting together some tracks. Kate looked at their overflowing in-box, looked at George, and then sighed.

By the end of the day, Kate had finished up their caseload and George had completed his model of the Silver Streak.

It was almost time to call it a day when the phone rang.

Kate answered the phone crisply. "Mathnet, Monday." She listened a moment. "Do we solve mysteries? Yes, we do. Do you have a mystery? I see . . . uh-huh. What's the address? We'll be right there."

"A mystery, Kate?" George asked, finally looking up from his train set.

"That was a young man named Walter Treppling."

"And what's his problem?"

"He says his house is haunted, George," Kate said. "Let's roll."

George gulped. "Haunted?"

Kate nodded. "Let's roll," she repeated, heading for the door. She didn't see her partner turn pale with dread.

An hour later, the Mathnet squad car was weaving its way through late-afternoon traffic in a small California town. George turned off the busy road onto a winding side street, and finally found their destination—123 Residual Drive.

"I thought you said this was a haunted house," George said to his partner as he drove through a set of tall iron gates and parked the car in the circular driveway. "This isn't a house. It's a *mansion.*"

A four-story house loomed against the sky, blocking the sunset. Along its walls, rosebushes grew in bright clumps against a strip of decorative tiles. Row after row of windows gazed out over the lawn, and fancy columns framed the oversized front door. George and Kate left the car and headed for the steps.

"This house is huge," George said, impressed. "In fact, this place is—"

"—falling apart," Kate yelped as her foot crashed through a rotten wood step.

George steadied his partner. Then he looked more closely at the house, noticing for the first time the missing tiles, overgrown flower beds, and creaking shutters. Even some of the windows were broken. "It could use a little paint," he agreed.

Just then the door opened. A pale young man peered around the edge of the door. He smiled nervously as George and Kate flashed their badges.

"Hello, I'm Kate Monday," said Kate, carefully maneuvering the rotten steps. "And this is my partner, George—"

"Frankly, Mathnet," George finished.

"Thank you for coming right away." The young man looked relieved. "I'm Walter Treppling." He invited them into the dark, dusty hallway.

The three stared at each other in silence for a minute.

"You said your house was haunted, Walter?" Kate prompted.

"It sure is," Walter said, looking nervous again.

"That's what has me scared. Little Louie is scared, too."

"Louie's your little brother?" George guessed.

Walter shook his head, his long blond bangs flopping in his face.

"Louie's my ward," he said.

"Your *ward*?" Kate asked.

"Yep."

Kate stared at Walter. "Aren't you a little young to have a ward?"

Walter shrugged. "I'm thirteen years old."

"Walter, is this your house?" George asked, looking around.

"Yes. Well, no. Well . . . sort of."

"Want to run that by us again?" Kate suggested.

"Sure, Ms. Monday." Walter took a deep breath, and started again. "See, I live next door, but ever since Mr. Tissue died, I've taken care of Louie."

"You mean Louie owns this house now?" Kate asked.

"Yes," said Walter. "Mr. Tissue left it to him in his will."

"Tissue . . . Tissue . . . " George was muttering. He paused. "You mean Roscoe 'Fatty' Tissue, the old vaudeville comic and semi-famous film luminary?" he suddenly asked.

"That's right, Mr. Frankly," Walter said, happy that George recognized his friend's name.

"Fatty Tissue lived *here*?" George asked in a starstruck tone and grinned, his face glowing. He was a big fan of vaudeville comedians. He loved their bad jokes and corny slapstick humor.

"When Fatty died, he left the house to his best friend, Little Louie, and he made me Louie's guardian," Walter continued.

"Where is Louie?" Kate asked.

"He's probably in his cage," Walter replied.

George frowned. "Walter, these things you're telling us . . . "

"Yes, sir?"

". . . aren't making any sense," Kate finished.

"Rats," Walter said. "And I haven't even told you about the ghosts yet."

"Why is Louie in a cage?" Kate asked. She was determined to get to the bottom of the problem.

"Little Louie's a parrot," Walter explained.

Kate was astonished. "Walter, you're telling us that you're the guardian of a *parrot?*"

"A parrot *owns* this house?" George asked, equally astonished.

"Yep. I come over two or three times a day to feed Little Louie and talk with him," Walter said. "We run a few lines, do shtick—"

"He means they tell each other jokes," George explained to Kate.

"Thanks, George," Kate said, glaring at her partner.

"Would you like to meet Louie?" Walter asked.

"More than anything else in the world," Kate said.

Walter led them through dim, winding hallways. Cobweb-covered marble statues and old portraits lined the walls.

"Fatty must have bought all this stuff during vaudeville's golden years," George said.

"Looks like those golden years have tarnished," Kate said, sneezing from all the dust.

"Fatty was a famous comic in the old days." Walter defended his friend. "But he retired from show business years ago. He didn't have any family. I used to come over and listen to him talk about the good old days. Then he and Little Louie would perform, and sometimes I'd join in with them."

Walter stopped in front of a set of doors. "The Drawing Room," he announced grandly, throwing the doors open.

The room wasn't as dilapidated as the rest of the house. In fact, it was a showplace. A leather wing chair and ottoman stood on the fancy oriental rug in front of a roaring fire. The bookshelves were crammed with books, and a small grand piano stood in a corner. Above the fireplace was a brilliant modern painting of multi-colored squares.

But the most interesting thing in the room was the cage hanging from the ceiling.

"That's where Little Louie lives," Walter said proudly.

"Wow! Does he *ever* live," George remarked. He peeked inside.

"A leather chair . . . a fireplace, a piano . . . " George blinked. "It's a miniature version of this room!"

"A perfect copy," Walter said, smiling for the first time.

"Pretty impressive," Kate said. "That grand piano—does it work?"

"Oh, sure, Ms. Monday," Walter said. He reached into the cage and plonked a few notes. "Everything works. And it's all to one-twelfth scale. Even that painting is one-twelfth the size of the original over there."

"That's pretty tiny," Kate commented.

George nodded. "Let's see, one twelfth as long and one twelfth as wide, so the total area of the cage is one hundred forty-fourth the size of the room."

Walter nodded in approval. "Mr. Tissue was a real freak when it came to scaling, too, Mr. Frankly."

"Bet he'd have loved your trains, George," Kate teased. She peered into the cage again. "Louie's home *is* amazing, but there seems to be something missing."

"Something missing?" George squeaked. "Are you kidding, Kate? He's got easy chairs, a library, a piano." He squinted into the cage. "Even a hi-fi set-up . . . "

"It's a CD player, actually," Walter bragged.

"Little Louie's got it all, Kate," George said. "What could be missing?"

"Little Louie, George," Kate said.

George looked around. Kate was right. He could see neither hide nor feather of the parrot.

"I'll call him," Walter said. He cleared his throat,

then called, "Little Louie, who was that lady I saw you with last night?"

"AWWWK!" They heard an ear-splitting squawk. Then a squeaky voice replied, "That was no lady, that was my wife!"

They turned, and there was Little Louie, perched on the head of a suit of armor in the corner of the drawing room. He fluffed his feathers as the threesome walked over to him. Louie was a large green parrot with a long red-and-blue tail. He cocked one bright yellow eye at them. George was sure he saw a smile on the big hooked beak.

"Hello, Little Louie," Walter greeted the bird. He smiled at Kate's and George's puzzled faces. "That's how I call Little Louie," he explained. "He learned every routine Mr. Tissue ever did. He loves jokes."

Louie took the cue. "I had a friend who was so fat, when he sat around the house, he sat *around* the house. Awwwk. Awwwk."

Kate groaned, but George looked at the bird in admiration.

"That's my kind of bird," George said. "Tell us another joke, Louie."

"Awwwwk! 1-1-2-3." the parrot said.

George scratched his head. "I don't know that one."

"This is all very interesting," Kate said, getting back to business. "But what does it have to do with ghosts and haunted houses?"

"That just started, Ms. Monday," Walter said. The nervous look was back on his face. "Lately, when I come over at night to tuck Louie into bed, I've been hearing these weird noises."

"Have you checked them out, Walter?" George asked, looking a little nervous himself.

"Well, not really . . . see . . . I tell myself there are no such things as ghosts."

Kate nodded. "And you're right, Walter."

"But most of the time, I don't believe myself," Walter admitted, hanging his head.

Louie squawked from his perch.

Kate ignored him. "Walter, there's no such thing as a ghost. There must be some other explanation. What exactly did the noises sound like?"

Walter thought a moment. "They sounded like—"

Suddenly, an eerie moaning filled the house. It echoed down the long hallways and seemed to come from everywhere at once. Above their heads came the noise of chains rattling and slow, heavy footsteps dragging across the floor.

Walter gulped. "They sounded like that!"

Just then, the lights went out.

DUM DE DUM DUM

CHAPTER
2

The Mathnetters stared at each other in the dim light of the flickering fireplace. Walter ran over to the piano and lit some candles in the candelabra that stood on the polished instrument.

"Good idea, Walter," Kate said. "Now we'll have some light while we investigate."

"Investigate?" George said in a shaky voice. "I don't know if that's such a good idea."

"What if the ghost gets us?" Walter asked, sounding scared.

"There are no such things as ghosts," Kate repeated. "Right, George?"

"Uh, right. But why don't we investigate tomorrow, when it's a little . . . brighter," George suggested.

Kate sighed. She grasped the candelabra firmly and led the way out of the room. In the hallway, she paused by a stairway as the moaning rose to a wild wail. "It's definitely coming from upstairs," she said.

Walter whispered, "Something's up there, I tell you."

Suddenly, a dark shape flew through the air, directly at George. The Mathnetter let out a yell and ducked.

"Look out! A ghost!" he shouted as the shape swooped by him.

"It's just Little Louie," Walter explained. "He goes to high places when he's afraid."

From the top of a crystal chandelier, Louie watched them with a laughing yellow eye. "Nevermore . . . nevermore . . . nevermore . . . Awwwk," he called.

George laughed weakly. "I knew it was him. I was just kidding. Heh. Heh. Heh."

Kate shook her head and turned to Walter. "How many rooms are on the second floor?" she asked.

"Six, Ms. Monday."

Kate took candles from the candelabra and handed them to Walter and George. "Let's go up," she said in a determined voice. "It's time to expose our 'ghost.'"

Walter followed Kate up the steps. George lagged behind.

"Come on, George," Kate said impatiently. "What's the matter?"

"I was just thinking, Kate," George said. He dawdled on the bottom step. "There are six rooms, so the probability of picking the right room on the first try is one in six—not very high."

"Are you afraid of ghosts, Mr. Frankly?" Walter asked.

"Of course not, Walter. There are no such things as ghosts." George looked nervously at the darkness beyond the candleglow. "It's just that when you're trying to solve a problem, it's good to examine all the possibilities—"

"Come on, George!" Kate interrupted. George reluctantly started up the stairs. He had gone only four steps when he stopped again.

"Of course, if we each take a room, our chances are three in six—three times greater," he figured.

"George!"

This time George made it all the way to the second floor. He was just about to bring up the subject of probability again, when Kate suddenly put a finger to her lips.

"Sssshhhhhh," she whispered. She surveyed the layout of the rooms. "We'll each take a room. When I give the signal, we'll each open a door."

When everyone was in position, Kate nodded, and the three doors were opened simultaneously.

"Ah-ha!" George said, leaping into his room, waving his candle wildly.

The room was empty. So were the rooms that Kate and Walter were exploring.

Kate shrugged, and pointed out each person's assignment for the next try. George opened his door—

nothing. Walter opened his door—nothing. Kate tried
to open her door, but it was jammed.

"Help me," she said to George as another groan
rumbled through the house. "I think this is where the
sounds are coming from."

George hesitated. Walter stepped up next to Kate
and helped her push. Nothing happened. Finally
George took a deep breath and added his shoulder to
the effort. The door opened a bit, but then was

slammed shut. "Somebody is in there!" Kate exclaimed.

"Or some *thing*," George muttered, but he pushed again. Push came to shove. With one great lunge, the threesome won the battle, the door burst open, and a heavy dark shape went somersaulting backward, groaned, and shook its mangy head.

"Well, well, well . . . if it isn't our 'ghost,'" said Kate.

Glaring at them through the semi-darkness was a big, unkempt man wearing dirty clothes with a filthy shirt that barely covered his bulging belly. He looked like he hadn't shaved in weeks.

Little Louie flew into the room and was the first to speak. "1-1-2-3."

George was distracted from the unexpected "ghost." He stared at Louie with a puzzled expression. "Why do you keep saying that?" George asked.

Kate elbowed her partner. They had a job to do. "What is your name, Mr. Ghost?" she asked sternly.

"Norman," the man grunted. He scratched his belly with one huge hand.

"First or last?" George asked, sounding as official as he could.

"First," Norman snarled.

"Want to try for a last?" George snarled back.

Norman wasn't impressed. "Tedge. Norman Tedge."

Kate continued the questioning. "Why are you trespassing in this house, Mr. Tedge?"

"You're the ones trespassing, not me," Tedge grumbled. "My uncle used to own this house."

"Fatty Tissue was your uncle?" George asked in amazement.

Tedge's eyes shifted guiltily. He backed down a bit. "Well, he was my great-uncle or something."

"He *never* mentioned your name to me," Walter declared. Now that he knew there wasn't a ghost, he was feeling much braver. "And you're not in Fatty's will. I know, I've seen it. It only talks about me and Little Louie."

"Want to try an explanation?" Kate asked.

"Okay, okay," Tedge shrugged, exposing more of his hairy stomach. "Fatty Tissue had an aunt who was a cousin to a woman who knew my mother, okay? I figure that makes me some kind of distant relative."

"I think you're reaching, Mr. Tedge," Kate said.

"I know Fatty Tissue left a fortune. I came to find it and claim it." Pointing to Louie, who was perched on a coat rack in the corner, Tedge added, "I deserve this house more than that molting bag of feathers over there."

"Shticks and shtones can break my bones . . . 1-1-2-3, AWWWK," was Louie's response.

"What makes you think Fatty Tissue had a fortune, Mr. Tedge?" George asked. "This house is practically falling apart. It doesn't look like Fatty died a millionaire."

"I'm telling you, I've checked it out," Tedge said. "Fatty made plenty of money. He had a great agent who cut beautiful deals for him."

"What kinds of deals?" Kate asked suspiciously.

"On his last three pictures, he got a hundred percent of the gross." Tedge said.

"One hundred percent of the gross?" George shook his head. "That's everything!"

"He made it big, and he didn't spend it. So it's got to be somewhere—probably right in this house," Tedge declared. He stopped scratching his stomach and started picking his big yellow teeth.

Kate was angry and getting angrier. "So you were trying to scare Walter away so you could find the money?"

Tedge nodded happily. "Yes, call me a hopeless romantic, but I love treasure hunts."

Walter glared at Tedge. Kate and George glared at Tedge. Even Little Louie glared at Tedge. Tedge just smirked.

Kate decided to wipe the smile off his face. "We're going to let you go this time, Mr. Tedge," she snarled, "but don't show up around here again, or you'll be looking down the barrel of a warrant for your arrest for trespassing. Now get out!"

"Yeah, get out," George added, pointing toward the door.

With a sneer on his lip and egg on his face, Norman Tedge slithered toward the door.

"Yeah, so long, sweetie," Little Louie said. As a parting shot, he buzzed Tedge's balding head and let out one of his ear-splitting squawks. Tedge hurried out, ducking and waving his arms.

"Well, that was easy," George said, dusting off his hands and looking pleased with himself.

"Maybe too easy," Kate said. She looked out the window and saw the bulky man shake a fist at the house. "I don't think we've seen the last of Norman Tedge."

DUM DE DUM DUM

CHAPTER

3

The next morning Kate entered Mathnet HQ to find George at his desk staring at some papers. She was just in time to see him give a huge yawn. Naturally, Kate yawned, too.

"Morning, George," she said when the yawning attack ended. "I didn't get nearly enough sleep last night."

"Me neither, Kate," George said. He rattled the papers in his hand. "But this should wake us up. Take a look."

"What is it?" Kate asked.

"It's Fatty Tissue's will. Walter gave me a copy last night. But I don't get this part. It says 'Walter, this is for you to puzzle out,' and then there's this picture."

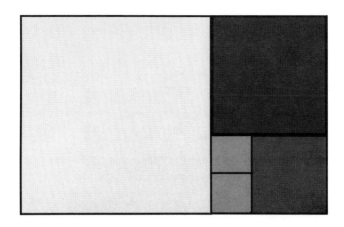

"Puzzle out?" Kate went to look over George's shoulder. "What an odd picture. It's just a bunch of squares."

"What do you make of it, Kate?" George asked, frowning.

"I don't know, George. It looks like some kind of pattern."

George picked up a ruler. "Look at the dimensions of these squares, Kate. 1 inch, 1 inch, 2, 3, 5." Before Kate could respond, the phone rang. George answered.

"Mathnet, Frankly." Suddenly, he sat up straighter. "Are you sure? Okay, we'll be right there."

"Walter Treppling again?" Kate guessed.

George nodded. "None other."

They headed for the door. "Another ghost?" Kate asked.

"Worse," George said grimly. "A missing person ... or avis, to be exact. Little Louie has flown the coop!"

When Kate and George arrived at Fatty's mansion, Walter met them at the door. He looked worried again. "When I came over to feed Louie his breakfast, he was gone," he cried.

Kate put a reassuring arm around the boy. "It's all right, Walter. We'll find him. Have you looked all over?"

"I've looked everywhere!" Walter wailed.

"Has Little Louie ever disappeared before?" George asked.

"Well . . . yes." Walter looked a little embarrassed. "Maybe I shouldn't have called you."

Kate shrugged. "We may as well help you look for him, as long as we're here."

They looked over the house carefully, calling out to Little Louie. He was nowhere to be found. Finally, they tried the backyard.

"This place is a jungle," George said, hacking his way through the overgrown garden. It was full of chest-high weeds and surrounded by tall trees and a huge wall so covered with ivy that you could hardly see it.

"Here, Little Louie. Polly want a cracker." George led the search party, calling out to the missing parrot.

Walter shook his head. "Little Louie won't answer to those kinds of things, Mr. Frankly. You've got to give him straight lines."

"Straight lines?" Kate asked.

"The setup lines for jokes," Walter explained. "Like this." He cupped his hands around his mouth and called, "Why did the parrot cross the road? If he's around and hears a setup, he'll yell the punch line right back." Walter cocked his head, listening for a response. There was only silence.

"Oh, I get it," George said, getting it. "Like, why does a fireman wear suspenders? To keep his pants up. Heh-heh-heh."

Walter corrected him. "No, Mr. Frankly, just the setup lines, Louie will give us the punch line. That's how we might find him."

The threesome spread out, calling out setup lines to old jokes.

"How do you make a bandstand?" No response.

"Take away their chairs," George whispered.

"What did the Roquefort say to the salad?" Nothing.

"Shut the refrigerator door; I'm dressing," George muttered.

"What time is it when an elephant steps on your watch?"

"Time to get a new watch," said George.

"George!" Walter and Kate both yelled.

"Sorry," George said sheepishly.

"Isn't there something else you could be doing?"

Kate asked.

George shrugged. Then he remembered the copy of Fatty's will he'd stuck in his pocket. While Kate and Walter continued the search for Louie, George studied the odd square drawing Fatty had made. He looked at it sideways, upside down, then right side up, and suddenly a light bulb seemed to go on in his head.

"Wait just a darned minute," said George. "Walter, what were those numbers Little Louie used to recite?"

"Uhh . . . 1-1-2-3."

"That's what I thought," said George. Then he called out, "1-1-2-3 . . . 1-1-2-3 . . . 1-1-2-3."

From a back corner of the estate grounds, from high up, they heard Louie yell, "5! Eureka!" Walter, Kate, and George looked into the treetops, relieved at hearing Louie's call. They saw Louie safe and sound, perched comfortably in a tree.

Louie flew to Walter's shoulder and nipped playfully at Walter's ear. Walter was grinning and giggling as he rubbed the parrot's brilliant green feathers. Louie squawked, "AWWWK! There's no place like home. There's no place like home."

Laughing, Walter suddenly remembered the sequence. "Mr. Frankly, what are those numbers, anyway?" he asked.

"They're the beginning of Fibonacci's number sequence," George said.

"Of course," Kate said, remembering her training

at Mathnet University.

"Fib-a-who-cheese?" asked Walter, who'd never been to Mathnet University.

George was only too happy to explain. "Fibonacci was an Italian mathematician who lived during the thirteenth century and had fun with numbers. He's known for a sequence of numbers starting with 1,1, in which the sum of the preceding two numbers adds up to the next number."

"Huh?" Walter said, frowning.

"Well, let's start with Louie's Fibonacci sequence," Kate said. "It begins with 1-1-2. 1 plus 1 equals 2. "

"And 1 and 2 is 3," Walter nodded, remembering that the next number in Louie's sequence was 3.

George took the next one. "And 2 and 3 is—"

"5! Eureka!" Louie added, as they all laughed.

"1, 1, 2, 3, 5," Walter recited. "It's great that you know about Fibo . . . Fido . . that guy's sequence and all, Louie, but why'd you learn to say that?"

Louie wasn't talking.

"And why did *you* suddenly guess that those numbers were the beginning of a sequence?" Kate asked her partner.

Unlike Louie, George was glad to explain. "What reminded me of it was this page I found in Fatty Tissue's will," he said. He showed the drawing to Kate and Walter.

George pointed to the five squares in the drawing.

"See, the five squares measure 1 inch, 1 inch, 2 inches, 3 inches, and 5 inches. 1-1-2-3-5!"

"Gee, I forgot about that part of the will," Walter said. "I *thought* it must be some kind of mathematical puzzle. We used to do them all the time. Mr. Tissue loved mathematics."

Kate had been staring hard at the drawing, too. "You know something, Pard," she said in a thoughtful tone. "That square pattern looks very familiar."

"I know what you mean, Ms. Monday," said Walter.

George nodded. "It looks exactly like — "

"The painting!" they all shouted at once.

With Little Louie riding on Walter's shoulder, the three of them strode purposefully into the house, into the drawing room, and up to the modern painting above the fireplace. They stared at the painting on the wall and the miniature in Little Louie's cage.

"That painting must be a clue to where the money is hidden," George said.

"You're right, partner," Kate agreed. "Otherwise, why would Fatty draw a picture of it in his will *and* teach Louie that sequence?"

"But where's the money?" Walter asked.

They shook their heads in puzzlement. Then Kate snapped her fingers. She reached up and very gently pulled the painting away from the wall.

"Look, a wall safe," Walter said in amazement. "Just like in bad movies."

"Fatty must have put his money in the safe," Kate said. She turned to Walter. "You don't happen to have the combination, do you?"

"No, I'm afraid I don't." Walter shook his head sadly.

"1,1,2,3,5!" Little Louie supplied.

George shrugged. "Well, it's worth a try." He carefully dialed. "1. . . 1 . . . 2 . . . 3 . . . 5."

There was a loud click, and the safe door slowly swung open.

"Eureka!" said George.

DUM DE DUM DUM

CHAPTER
4

Kate and Walter held their breath as George reached inside. He removed the contents.

"That's *it*?" Kate asked in disbelief. "*A tape recorder*?!"

"Mr. Tissue used these a lot," Walter said, hiding his own disappointment. "Let's push Play."

Walter pressed the button. As the tape played, they heard a scratchy sound, followed by Fatty's voice. Fatty's voice was scratchy, too. He sounded a bit like W. C. Fields:

> "If you found this, Walter,
> I'm as happy as can be.
> Listen to Little Louie.
> He can lead you to the key."

George whispered, "It sounds like another puzzle." The tape continued:

> "Remember what you just learned,
> And don't turn up your noses.
> Look for number patterns,
> And stop and smell the roses.
> Good luck, Walter."

"That's the end," Kate said when the scratching sound began again.

Walter turned off the tape. He gathered up Little Louie and put him gently in his cage. He locked the cage door. "I told you Mr. Tissue was a real puzzle lover," he said.

"He sure was," George said. "Let's listen one more time." He rewound the tape and pushed Play.

> "If you found this, Walter,
> I'm as happy as can be."

"Stop," Kate said. "Okay, Fatty knows that if Walter is listening to this tape recording, he has obviously solved the first part of the puzzle."

They all nodded. George pushed Play again.

> "Listen to Little Louie.
> He can lead you to the key."

George pushed Stop and looked at Little Louie, who didn't say a word. The parrot just perched in his easy chair and stared off into space, blinking his yellow eyes in an innocent way.

"You're a big help, Louie!" George said. He pushed Play again.

> "Remember what you just learned,
> And don't turn up your noses."

George stopped the tape and asked Kate and Walter, "What have we just learned?"

Kate and Walter answered in unison, "Fibonacci!"

George started the tape for Fatty's last lines:

> **"Look for number patterns,
> And stop and smell the roses.
> Good luck, Walter."**

There was a moment's pause, then Kate said, "The Fibonacci sequence *is* a number pattern. . . . "

"And stop and smell the roses means slow down," George said, "take some time, appreciate life—" Suddenly George interrupted himself. "—Kate! Stop and smell the roses!"

"What are you talking about, George?"

"There are rosebushes right in front of this house!"

In no time at all, Kate, George, and Walter were outside, pawing their way through the rosebushes that were growing by the tile wall by the side of the driveway. For many long, thorny moments they found nothing but row after row of plain, identical tiles when they pulled back the dead and dying bushes. Then George shoved one large bush out of the way revealing several different, darker-colored tiles arranged in a pattern.

"1,1,2,3,5." He counted off the darker squares. "Look! The Fibonacci sequence. 1-1-2-3-5. The sequence is right here in the wall."

Kate moved in and pulled the roses back further so they could see some more of the wall. The strip of tiling was five tiles high at its highest point and stretched nineteen columns across.

George counted the tiles in each column. "3,3,1,4,5,4 . . ."

Kate added the new numbers onto the first five. "The sequence now reads 1-1-2-3-5-3-3-1-4-5-4-4-3-2-5-2-2-4-2," she said.

"But what does it mean?" George asked.

"Maybe it's *another* clue," Kate said with a weary sigh.

George grabbed a camera from the squad car and took some pictures of the wall for reference. "Ooops. I'm out of film. And I'd like to take a *few* more shots for us to study back at the office," he said.

"There's some film inside," Walter said. "I'll go get it."

A moment later, he was back, running out the door of the house, yelling, "Ms. Monday, Mr. Frankly . . . Little Louie . . . "

"What about him, Walter?" Kate asked, concerned.

"Little Louie is missing!" Walter gasped.

"Calm down, Walter," said George. "He's probably just flying around the backyard."

But Walter shook his head. He looked wild with worry. "No, this time he's really gone!" he cried. "Someone broke the lock on his cage. Little Louie's been birdnapped!"

DUM DE DUM DUM

CHAPTER
5

George and Kate calmed Walter down and went inside to examine the cage.

"You're right, Walter," George said when he had checked the lock. "It's clear the lock's been broken."

Someone had also bent the door and done some damage to the cage and its furnishings. It looked as if Louie hadn't gone without a fight.

Kate patted Walter on the shoulder. "You stay here in case Little Louie returns. We'll get back to Mathnet Headquarters and call this in. The number pattern will have to wait. Finding Little Louie is our top priority now."

In the squad car, Kate looked up pet shops in the special Mathnet business directory. It seemed like a good way to start. But after visiting six stores with no luck, they were getting discouraged. "Maybe 7 is our lucky number, Pard," Kate said hopefully. "The next shop is on the right, in the next block."

They parked in front of Birdlands, a shop owned by the famous big game hunter, Frank Puck. They entered and identified themselves, showing their badges.

Kate introduced herself. "I'm Kate Monday, and this is my partner, George—"

"—Frankly, Mathnet," George finished.

"How can I help?" Puck asked, leaning a muscular arm on the counter and staring intently at the Mathnetters.

"Do you specialize in birds, Mr. Puck?" George asked. Kate and Puck stared at him.

"Yes, all kinds of birds," said Puck.

George brightened. "Do you know how I can get rid of a gaggle of geese in my garage?"

"George!" Kate scolded. "Mr. Puck, we have reason to believe a valuable parrot has been stolen."

"It happens all the time." Puck shook his head sorrowfully. "Parrots make good companions. There's always a demand for them."

"Has anyone offered to sell you a parrot in the past few hours?" George asked, back to business.

"No." Puck shrugged. "A man came by with a myna bird about fifteen minutes ago."

"But no parrot?"

"Sorry," Puck said. "Can you describe the bird?"

George held out his hands. "He's about this tall and covered with feathers."

Kate added, "His name is Little Louie, and—"

"Little Louie?" Puck asked in dismay. "Fatty Tissue's bird?"

"Yes," George said. "Do you know Little Louie?"

"We've never met, but I know *of* him," Puck said. "He's probably the most famous parrot in show biz."

"Really?" Kate asked.

"What a talent." Puck looked dreamily into space. "Have you ever heard him sing *Madame Butterfly*?"

"No," George admitted.

"It would break your heart. I hope nothing un-birdlike has happened to him." Puck sounded concerned.

"If you hear anything, Mr. Puck, please give us a call."

"You bet I will."

Back in the squad car, Kate and George got a message from Dispatch. They had put out an additional APB to all taxidermy shops when Little Louie showed up missing.

"A man from one of the taxidermy stores just called," said Dispatch. "He said someone brought in a dead parrot to be stuffed and mounted about an hour ago." Dispatch gave them information on the shop.

George and Kate exchanged grim looks and drove back to Residual Drive to pick up Walter. It would be a gruesome job, but a relative had to be present to make a positive ID. Walter was the only family Louie had.

No one spoke in the squad car as the threesome headed toward Mel's Taxidermy & Card Shoppe. Kate had phoned ahead to explain the situation. They were greeted at the door by a large, cadaverous-looking man dressed as an undertaker, complete with a string tie. His skin looked as though it had not seen sunlight in several decades.

"Hellllooooo," said the man. "I'm Mel. Welllllcoooooome."

George and Kate flashed their badges, and Mel gestured them inside.

"This waaaaay." Mel led them past stuffed animals, antlers, and tables crowded with weird instruments and jars of strange liquids. The sound of organ music in the background was punctuated only by the shuffle of their shoes on the tile floor. George was tight-lipped, Kate felt her skin crawl, and Walter was near tears.

"This is the Moooooorgue." Mel opened a door. The room was lined with metal filing cabinets of different sizes and dominated by a large metal table in the center with a stack of clean towels at one end. Mel consulted the note in his hand.

"Aaaaaah. Number Fooooour." Mel walked to a cabinet. He counted down four drawers and motioned George, Kate and especially Walter to come closer. He opened the drawer slowly, revealing a small white sheet covering the remains of a parrot. One claw stuck out the bottom with a cardboard tag tied to it. Mel snapped back the sheet.

"Aaargh!" George looked away. "Poor Louie!"

Walter was peering closely at the still form. He heaved a great sigh. "It's not Louie, Mr. Frankly. It's some other bird."

As they drove away from Mel's, the atmosphere was a bit cheerier. Walter and George even told each other a few bad jokes. Then Kate pointed out that they'd better get back to business. "We seem to be getting nowhere fast. We need more information to solve this crime."

"Who would have reason to birdnap Little Louie?" George wondered aloud.

There was quiet in the squad car as they all thought for a minute.

"Do you suppose it could be that fake ghost, Tedge?" Walter wondered.

"It could be, Walter. Good thinking." Kate checked her notes and announced, "It so happens he lives quite near here. Let's pay a little surprise visit on Norman Tedge."

George pulled into a driveway to turn around, and before long they were cruising slowly through a run-down section of town looking for Tedge's address. They found it and parked.

"No wonder he wants to find Fatty's fortune," George said, as they picked their way through overturned trash cans, broken glass and other debris to Tedge's apartment building. On the side of a brick wall was a faded sign that read, *Post Some Bills - Please.*

They walked up two flights of stairs and found the

door to apartment 3B. George knocked four times on the door: "Dum de dum dum."

"Who is it?" snarled a familiar voice.

"Frankly, Mathnet. Open up, Tedge. We want to ask you some questions."

"Just a minute. I'm . . . I'm not dressed."

They heard some brief scuffling noises inside, but then the door opened, revealing Norman Tedge, dressed just as shabbily as he had been the other day. He greeted Walter and the Mathnetters with a grumpy "Yeah?"

"You dress in a hurry, Mr. Tedge," Kate observed, moving into the room.

"I have fast clothes, Ms. Monday. What do you want?"

George and Walter entered, and they all looked around. The place was a shambles. There was a single mussed-up bed, and newspapers were strewn about. A bottle of milk stood half-full and sour-looking, next to a bowl of what looked like gravel. A radio with a coat hanger as an antenna was set on an orange crate. A single bare light bulb was the total source of light, since the cracked and torn window shade was down. In short, the place looked perfectly awful.

"Just out of curiosity, Mr. Tedge, what do you do for a living?" George asked.

"I'm an interior decorator," Tedge said sarcastically. "But I'm sure you didn't come here to talk about my choice of drapes."

"No," Kate said firmly. "We came about a bird."

"A bird?" Tedge acted innocent. He didn't act very well.

"Little Louie, to be specific," George said.

"What about him?" Tedge asked.

Walter took a step toward Tedge. "Somebody stole him."

"And you think it was me?" Tedge sneered.

George corrected him. "You think it was *I*."

Tedge was puzzled. "I think it was you?"

Kate got things back on track. "We think you nabbed Little Louie," she said accusingly.

"Ridiculous," Tedge scoffed. He didn't scoff very well, either. "What would I want with a parrot?"

"I've heard they make good companions," George said.

"Mind if we look around?" Kate said, beginning to look around.

Tedge tried to get in her way. "Yes I *do* mind." For a moment it looked as if the Mathnetters would be forced to leave.

Walter picked up the bowl from the table. "Ms. Monday, Mr. Frankly, look! Birdseed!"

"That's not birdseed." Tedge grabbed the bowl. "Those are . . . stale Grape nuts. I love 'em. See?" He shoved a fistful in his mouth.

In the brief confusion, Kate had worked her way to the closet door. "Well, well, well," she said after opening it. "And how do you explain *this*?"

Inside was Little Louie, tied to a perch, with a gag taped around his beak.

Walter rushed to untie Louie, who was thrilled to be free. "How'd the chimpanzee escape from his cage?" he squawked. "With a *monkey* wrench! Aaawk!"

"Hello, Little Louie," George said.

"Eureka!" Louie shouted.

When everyone had calmed down, Kate got down to business. "Mr. Tedge, why did you birdnap Little Louie?" she asked.

"I thought he might tell me where Tissue's fortune is." Tedge shrugged. "I didn't hurt him."

Walter reached down into the closet and picked up a flashlight and a tiny rubber hammer. He waved them angrily under Tedge's nose. "Didn't hurt him, huh?"

"He gave me the third degree, he gave me the third degree." Louie shuddered and ruffled his feathers when he saw the hammer. "Awk!"

Tedge showed no signs of being sorry. "I just scared him a little, that's all," he said.

Kate picked up the telephone. "Mind if I use your phone, Mr. Tedge? I want to call for a backup unit and have you arrested."

"Be my guest," Tedge replied in a sneering voice.

"Hello?" Kate smiled as she watched George and Walter kidding around with Louie. Then her smile turned to a frown. She looked down at the receiver and clicked the buttons on the phone. "Operator? Operator?"

Kate hung up the phone. "It's dead," she said, looking around. "Don't you pay your phone bill, Mr. Tedge? Mr. Tedge?"

The door was open, and Tedge was gone.

DUM DE DUM DUM

CHAPTER
6

As soon as they returned to Mathnet HQ, Kate put out an APB on Norman Tedge. Walter set up a makeshift perch on a file cabinet for Little Louie. George began studying the blackboard, where he had drawn a reproduction of the tile pattern on Fatty's wall. After a moment, Kate joined him. She stared at the pattern.

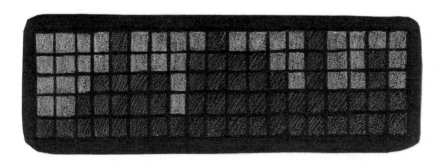

"George, maybe it's time to play What Do We Know?" Kate suggested.

Louie squawked, "What do we know, what do we

know. Sacramento is the capital of California . . . Awwk!"

Walter was curious. "How do you play What Do We Know?"

"It's a way of organizing facts, Walter," George said. "When you're trying to solve a problem, you can't afford to overlook anything."

Kate started. "Okay, we know Fatty had a fortune."

"Do we know that for sure, Kate?" George asked.

"Debbie checked it for us," Kate reported. "She said he netted more than twenty-five million dollars from his movies."

"Wow," Walter said. "That's a lot of cash."

"Big bucks, big bucks," added Louie.

"It sure is a lot of money." Kate threw up her hands. "But *where* is it?"

"Maybe he took it with him," George guessed. "You know . . . in the coffin."

"Debbie checked that out, too, George. Fatty was buried at Forest Lawn by the funeral home of Tinkerstoo Everstoo Fatchance. It was a simple ceremony, and there was nothing in the box but Fatty Tissue."

George had been doing some research, too. "I checked the banks. Nothing. *Then* I checked under aliases. You know, a.k.a., also known as, phony names."

Kate and Walter stared at George. He simply stared back.

"Well?!" Kate and Walter demanded.

"Well, nothing."

Kate tapped her pencil on the desk. "So we know he had a lot of money and it's probably somewhere in the house."

"*I* never saw it," said Walter.

"Walter, do you know of any other safes or hiding places where Fatty Tissue might have hidden something valuable?" George asked. Walter shook his head.

"Another thing we know is that Fatty loved numbers and mathematics," Kate said.

Pointing to the tile pattern on the blackboard, George added, "He sure did . . . complicated mathematics and puzzles."

Walter walked over to the board. "Like this one. Is it another Fibonacci sequence?"

"Nope," George said. "It starts out 1-1-2-3-5."

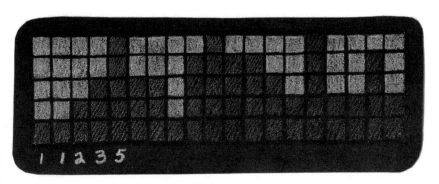

"But then it changes," Kate added.

"I see what you mean," Walter said. "Like this part. 3 and 3 don't equal 1. It doesn't make any sense."

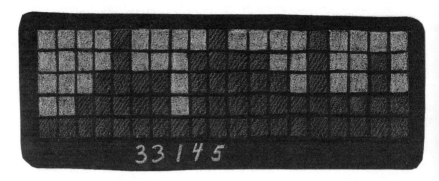

"Not yet, anyway," George said. "Let's keep working on it. It's a good way to solve a problem."

"And while you two do that," Kate said, heading for the phone, "I'll check Dispatch and see if they've had any luck catching up with Norman Tedge."

"Skin him alive. Tar and feathers are too good for him," Louie squawked from his perch. He ruffled his own feathers at the mere mention of the birdnapper's name.

At the board, Walter observed, "It *is* the same as the Fibonacci sequence to start, isn't it, Mr. Frankly?"

"It sure is, Walter."

Walter pointed.

"1 and 1 is 2 . . . 1 and 2 is 3," Walter muttered. "2 and 3 is 5 . . . "

"Uh-huh," George encouraged. "Go on."

"5 and 3 is 8. 8 tiles won't fit on the wall, will they, Mr. Frankly?"

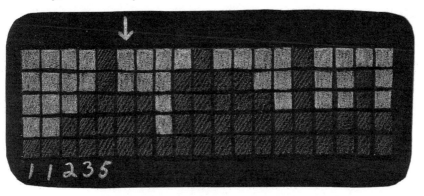

"No, they won't, Walter." George consulted the board. The tile strip was only 5 tiles high.

A few moments passed as George and Walter studied the diagram of the wall.

Then Walter said, "Unless you carry the remainder."

"Carry?"

"Like in adding," Walter explained. "When you have too many for the ones place, you carry over to the tens place and leave the remainder."

"Remainder? Carry?" George was grinning from ear to ear. "Walter, I think you've done it! Look at this. 1 and 1 is 2, 1 and 2 is 3, 2 and 3 is 5." He pointed at the tiles drawn on the board as he spoke, and wrote numbers under them.

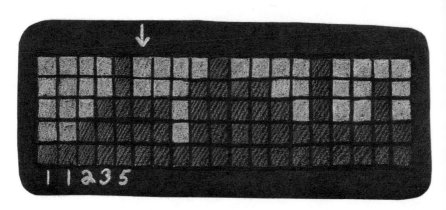

1 1 2 3 5

"But there are only enough tiles to go up to 5 in each column," George said. "So Fatty had to carry. Whenever he did that, he just put down the remainder."

"So say we have to add two numbers that add up to 8." Walter held up both hands, with three fingers sticking up on one hand, and five on the other. "8 means we'll have 3 more than 5—three more tiles than we'd be able to fit on the wall." George pointed.

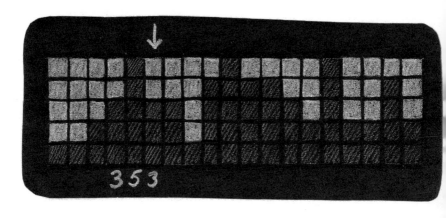

3 5 3

"So we'd put down the remainder, 3. And there are three tiles in this column," he said triumphantly.

Kate joined them at the board. "What are you two doing?"

George pointed to the next two numbers on the board. "Kate, look at this. See, here we add the two numbers 3 and 3. 3 plus 3 is—"

"Six," Walter said.

"So?" Kate questioned.

George explained as he pointed to the tiles. "There isn't room for six tiles. So Fatty just put in the remainder. See, Kate, every time the count goes over 5, we only show the remainder."

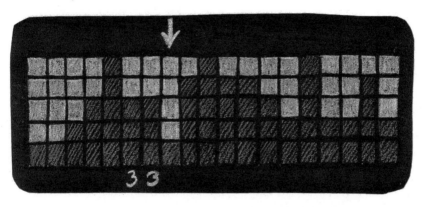

"I see," said Kate. She moved along the board to the next pair to be added. "So here, where we have to add 1 and 4, we put 5 in the next column, because 5 will fit. But then we have to add the 4 and 5. That means the next number is 9. But 9 won't fit. So we leave out 5 and just put down the remainder."

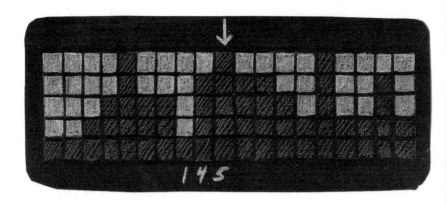

"Four!" Walter shouted.

"Right, Walter," George said. "And I think it works across the wall."

They all spent the next few minutes adding and carrying.

"5 and 4 is 9, remainder 4. 4 and 4 is 8, remainder 3," Walter muttered aloud as he figured. "4 and 3 is 7, remainder 2. 3 and 2 is 5, all 5 fit. 5 and 2 is 7, remainder 2 again. 2 and 2 is 4, 4 fits. Then 2 and 4 is 6, remainder . . . "

Walter stopped muttering and scratched his head. "Uh, this last column has an extra tile."

"You're right, Walter," George said. "That spoils the whole pattern."

George and Walter looked glum. They were so close!

But Kate was smiling. "Don't you see," she said, the pattern was a clue. And if there's a tile that doesn't belong, that might be where—"

Kate, George and Walter finished as one, "—FATTY HID THE TREASURE!"

"Eureka!" Little Louie squawked, in a way that seemed to say "I knew it all along."

It felt like the longest ride in history, as the four-some (including Louie, of course) aimed the Mathnet squad car through the city, over the bridge, along the highway, over country roads, down Residual Drive and up the driveway to Fatty Tissue's mansion. Car doors flew open as the car rocked to a stop. Walter and the Mathnetters stumbled over the dead rosebushes as they made a beeline for the wall. They paused a moment to catch their breath and carefully counted the last three columns, just to be certain.

"2 plus 4 is . . . " Kate began.

"Six," Walter finished.

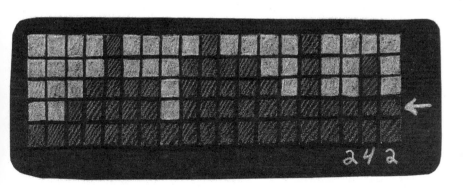

George pointed as he counted, "That should mean a remainder of 1."

"And there are two tiles," Walter said in triumph.

No one spoke as George got out his Swiss army knife and carefully pried loose the extra tile. He reached into the hole behind it.

Once again, Kate and Walter held their breaths. And once again they were disappointed.

"That's *it*? A *key*?" Kate said in disbelief.

"Not another puzzle," Walter moaned.

But George had been reading a tag attached to the key. "Not another puzzle and not just any old key," he said. "It's a key to a safety deposit box at The Next to the Last National Bank, and the tag says 'Box 313, property of Walter Treppling.'"

Louie squawked, "Eureka!"

"Eureka is right, let's roll," Kate said. "We've got a vault to check out."

At the bank, they identified themselves and showed the teller the key. They were ushered into the bank vault.

George was about to open safety deposit box 313 when he was overcome by the drama of the moment. He cleared his throat and made a speech:

"Kate, Walter, Louie, before I open this vault, I'd just like to take a moment to say that if it hadn't been for all of us, working together under very trying circumstances, and sticking it out trying to solve this very difficult mathematical problem, we'd probably never

have found ourselves on the brink of—"

"OPEN IT!!!" Kate, Walter, and Louie shouted.

"I was just getting to it," George said sheepishly.

Inside the box were stacks and stacks of cash. And another tape player.

They all stared at the money for a minute, then George gestured to the tape machine. "I think you should do the honors, Walter."

Walter pushed the Play button.

"Good evening, ladies and germs."

It was, without a doubt, the raspy voice of Roscoe "Fatty" Tissue.

"Walter, in this box is enough money for you to get a very, very good college education. You've earned it. I want you to use it and learn. Learn as much as you can, because nobody can ever take that away from you. Good luck, Walter, and I'd like to say this to my fine-feathered friend, Little Louie—"

Louie said, "Go for it . . . Awk!"

The voice on the tape continued.

"Louie, did I ever tell you the one about the mathematician's toolbox? Ha, ha, ho, ho, hoooooeeeeey . . . "

Fatty's taped laughter was so infectious that they all began to laugh. They all did high fives with each other, except for Little Louie, who did high feathers, and finished the joke:

"It was full of multi-pliers! AWK!"

DUM DE DUM DUM

EPILOGUE

Norman Tedge was picked up by the ever-vigilant Los Angeles Police Department while walking *near* the Beverly Hills Hotel without permission or white shoes. He was convicted of a 487F, grand theft feathers, and caged away from society until he began to molt.

DUM DE DUM DUM

ACTIVITIES

BIRDSEED FOR SCALE!

Little Louie, the parrot, lives in a cage that is a scaled-down version of the drawing room. Louie's cage is built on one-twelfth scale—everything is exactly one-twelfth the size of the larger room.

1. To celebrate solving the case, Kate and George want to buy Louie some of his favorite gourmet birdseed. They want to make sure the box they choose is exactly one-twelfth scale. A real box measures 12 inches, by 6 inches, by 3 inches. Look at the birdseed boxes below. Which box is one-twelfth scale?

BOX A   BOX B

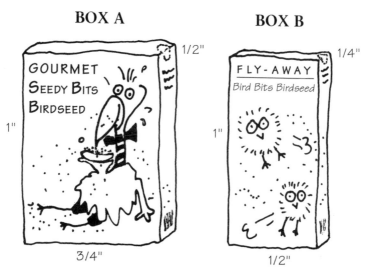

2. Louie may like his Gourmet Seedy Bits Birdseed served in little boxes, but sometimes he has a bigger appetite than that. He can actually eat one half of a large box of birdseed measuring 12 inches, by 6 inches, by 3 inches. Which box below can hold exactly one half the amount of birdseed as the large box? Remember volume is measured by multiplying height times length times width.

BOX A

BOX B

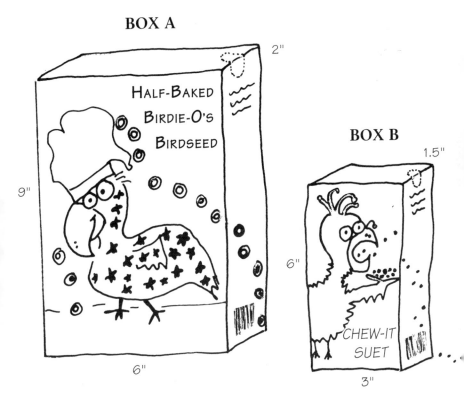

FATTY'S FIBONACCI

Fatty Tissue used the Fibonacci sequence as the combination to his safe. This sequence of numbers was discovered by a mathematician, who amazingly had the same name—Fibonacci. (Well, maybe it's not so amazing since they named it for him.) In a Fibonacci series you start by adding one to one—the first two numbers in the series—to get two. Then you add one to two to get three. Now your series reads 1, 1, 2, 3 . . . and will go on as long as you keep adding the last two numbers in the series.

Fibonacci's sequence begins with one and one. But a Fibonacci-like sequence can start with *any* two same numbers. Like 2 and 2 or 6 and 6.

1. Suppose you knew that the safe combination was a Fibonacci-like sequence that ended with 20, 32, 52. Could you find the four numbers that begin the series? What are they?

2. Here's another problem. Suppose Louie starts reciting a combination but instead of saying some of the numbers, he whistles one note for every missing number. The sequence comes out like this: whistle, whistle, 6, whistle, 15.

What are the three missing numbers?

IT'S A MODULAR, MODULAR, MODULAR WORLD

Kate and George had trouble following the Fibonacci sequence in the wall tiles because the tiles were only five rows high. They discover that the tiles represent a number system where five is the highest number. Every time a sum is greater than five, you must write down only the remainder. This kind of number system is called Modulo Five.

When adding in Modulo Five, if the sum is greater than five, you subtract five from the sum and write down the remainder. For example, 3 + 4 = 7. Since 7 is greater than 5, you subtract 5 from seven and you have a remainder of 2. Therefore, in a Modulo Five world, 3 + 4 = **2**.

1. What if Kate and George made a wall that was *seven* tiles high? If they started with the Fibonacci series 1,1,2,3,5, what would the next four numbers be?

2. What if they made a wall that was *six* tiles high? What would the next four numbers be?

ANSWERS

BIRDSEED FOR SCALE

1. Box B is one-twelfth scale.

2. Box A holds exactly half the volume.
Big box *volume* is 12 x 6 x 3 = 216 cubic inches.
Box A's volume is 9 x 6 x 2 = 108 cubic inches.
Box B is exactly half scale but the volume is
6 x 3 x 1.5 = 27 cubic inches.

FATTY'S FIBONACCI

1. 4, 4, 8, 12

(32 - 20 = **12**), (20 - 12 = **8**), (12 - 8 = **4**), (8 - 4 = **4**)

2. 3, 3, 6, 9, 15

The missing numbers are 3, 3, 9.

(15 - **9** = 6), (9 - 6 = **3**), (6 - 3 = **3**)

IT'S A MODULAR, MODULAR, MODULAR WORLD

1. If the wall is only seven tiles high, the next four numbers would be: 1, 6, 7, 6

[(3 + 5 = 8) - 7 = **1**], (5 + 1 = **6**), (1 + 6 = **7**), [(6 + 7 = 13) - 7 = **6**]

2. If the wall is only six tiles high, the next four numbers would be: 2, 1, 3, 4

[(3 + 5 = 8) - 6 = **2**], [(5 + 2 = 7) - 6 = **1**], (2 + 1 = **3**), (1 + 3 = **4**)